Murder in Three Movements

A Little Firling Mystery – Book Six

by Belinda Chavremootoo

Dedication

*For every cat who ever solved a mystery

quietly before the humans caught up.*

Text Copyright

Coming Soon: Murder in the Open Air

A Little Firling Mystery – Book Seven

"All the world's a stage, and all the men and women merely players."
— William Shakespeare, As You Like It

Twenty years ago, during a summer play in the village of Little Firling, a young actress vanished without a trace. Her disappearance was whispered about, then buried in silence.

Now, the same play is being performed again — with many of the same people, on the same stage, in the same place where it all went wrong. Retired professor Annabel didn't expect to become entangled in the production's secrets. But when a young man disappears, and someone starts rewriting the past in dangerous ways, she's left with no choice. As memories resurface and old wounds tear open, Annabel must unravel what really happened to the young actress — and why someone is so desperate to keep that story from being told.

With a determined heart, a sharp mind, and a cat who misses nothing, she steps into the spotlight of a tragedy still waiting for its final scene.

Because some truths refuse to stay
buried.

Table of Contents

Prologue

The first daffodils had come early that year.

Little Firling's hedgerows, usually hesitant in April, blushed yellow as though spring itself had something to prove.

Above the square, garlands fluttered like secrets — neatly knotted, lovingly looped, ready to welcome the festival crowds.

No one was watching the orchard.

No one ever did.

Once, it had been a place for children's games and summer apples.

Now it belonged to silence.

And to her.

She stood at the edge of the tree line, hands in her coat pockets, watching the sky shift. The same sky she'd looked up at, once, long ago, before things had gone wrong.

Before truth became something people buried alongside the dead.

She hadn't meant to come back.

But something had pulled her. A letter. A memory. A name said too softly to ignore.

Julian Parrish.

And just like that, the movements had begun.

One beat.

One fall.

One echo.

And now, one final truth waiting to be heard — among the blossoms, beneath the garlands, before the festival music began.

Not all flowers bloom in sunlight.

Some return for justice.

Chapter 1

The tulips were blooming early.

Annabel clipped a pale-yellow stem, cradling the bloom like a secret as she placed it in the basket beside the chives. The early daffodils had mostly faded now, but the tulips stood proud — a little smug in their symmetry — and the herb beds were already lively with green promise.

Near the back of the garden, her roses were stretching themselves awake.

The New Dawn was climbing gently along the trellis, new shoots twisting like sleepy arms. Desdemona sat beneath, quietly regal with her ghost-pale buds barely visible through the foliage. And Double Delight, ever the dramatic one, had already thrown out two spindly branches in defiance of the calendar.

"Not your time yet," Annabel murmured. "But I admire your spirit."

Persephone, settled on the garden bench with one paw dangling over the side, gave a slow blink as if to say *they'll do as they please. As should we all.*

***

Back in the cottage, the kitchen was warm and fragrant.

Annabel stirred lamb and cinnamon in the skillet, layering aubergines in a dish with quiet concentration. Moussaka was her stress dish — enough steps to focus her mind, enough comfort to soften her thoughts.

Persephone, unimpressed by the smell of garlic, had retreated to the windowsill, where she could judge both the pan and the weather in equal measure.

Just as Annabel slid the dish into the oven, the door burst open.

"Do you *have* any idea," Evie huffed, "how big the maypole is this year?"

She kicked off her boots, flung her coat over the back of a chair, and immediately helped herself to a slice of tomato from the counter.

Annabel didn't look up.

"You're dripping."

"I'm victorious. Minor detail."

"That's for layering," Annabel said flatly.

"It offended me with its smug curve. You'd have done the same."

Persephone let out a soft chuff and padded toward the hearth. Evie watched her like one might watch a suspicious local with gossip tucked in their sleeves.

"I'm telling you; this year's festival is *already* chaos. Yewling sent a team to weigh the maypole base. *Weigh it,* Annabel. It's not a trebuchet — it's a maypole."

Annabel raised an eyebrow.

"Friendly rivalry."

"Weaponized bunting," Evie muttered. "Nora nearly smacked Gareth with a tea tray."

***

The Spring Harmony Festival had begun.

Officially, it will kick off the next day. Unofficially, it had been brewing for weeks — schedules written and rewritten, wreaths measured, bunting counted with growing suspicion.

It was an annual event shared between Little Firling and Little

Yewling, and it brought out the *best* and *most ridiculous* in both.

Craftsmanship challenges. Cake judging. Sausage link competitions. Tug-of-war. The maypole ribbon dance. And, of course, the Harmony Cup — a battered silver vessel that no one remembered the origin of but everyone wanted on display in their village hall.

Little Firling was known for its charm. Its "character."

Little Yewling was known for its muscle and precision. And smugness.

Evie referred to them as *"the over-groomed under-smilers."*

This year, events were split: Little Firling handled *presentation and ceremony,* while Little Yewling took on *timing and infrastructure.*

A pairing that had *not* gone smoothly.

Annabel had overheard a fierce debate over *flower arch weight tolerances* behind the church. Two days ago, someone had "accidentally" loosened the signage on the Yewling sausage stall.

"It's war," Evie had declared over tea. "Polite war. But war."

***

Outside in the square, chaos bloomed with the garlands.

Children were trying (and failing) to learn the maypole dance, a small dog had stolen a practice ribbon and was running wild, and someone had replaced the Yewling sausage banner with a sign that said *"Firling Knows How to Link Properly."*

Mira Harrington handed out sugar buns like peace offerings.

Douglas Hartley was muttering about the load-bearing specs of the garland arch.

And Nora Cadwallader — armed with a clipboard and a spoon — was guarding the teacup tent like a wartime general.

"If Gareth *touches* that bunting again, I'm gluing his fingers together."

The Spring Harmony Festival wasn't just bunting and biscuits. It was bragging rights.

Julian Parrish stood at the centre of it all, charming, laughing, glowing like he personally invented spring.

He winked at the maypole dancers, adjusted a garland, and complimented the colour symmetry of a trellis no one else had even noticed yet.

"He's in his element," Annabel said, sipping herbal tea from a compostable cup.

"He's insufferable," Evie muttered. "And the garland's too low. He's going to trip someone."

Julian had won woodcarving three years in a row, tug-of-war twice, and even tossed the caber so cleanly last year that the judges had to make up new compliments.

He knew how to command a crowd, build a stall, string a garland without creasing it, and seduce a judge without saying a word.

And he knew he knew it.

Little Yewling adored him.

Little Firling tolerated him.

But both watched him.

Persephone, nestled under a nearby bench, flattened her ears as if in agreement.

***

By afternoon, the square pulsed with colour and anticipation.

The noise of the two villages mingled into something that sounded like *a choir rehearsing and arguing at the same time.*

Laughter bubbled up in bursts, tangled with the clatter of tent poles, the whistle of boiling kettles, and the distant bleat of someone's runaway goat.

And the smells—

Sugar glaze, fried onions, trampled grass, cinnamon, warm fudge, wet wool, and just enough floral perfume to declare war on bees.

Ribbons snaked from lampposts.

Garlands bloomed between stalls.

Children carried cones of ribbon for practice while their parents compared sponge textures and quietly rehearsed their competitive flower arranging.

And Julian Parrish?

He stood in the centre of it all, *charming, laughing, glowing* like he personally invented spring.

Annabel sipped her herbal tea and narrowed her eyes.

"He's really leaning into the ringleader role this year," she said.

"He's always leaned," Evie muttered. "Mostly on other people's nerves."

Persephone sat beneath the lemonade table, ears flat, tail flicking like punctuation.

***

Later that afternoon, Julian climbed into the central tent — the massive one that housed the garland showcase and anchored the maypole at its heart.

He adjusted a ribbon. Smoothed a knot. Shouted a joke to the crowd.

Someone laughed. Someone else scowled.

A breeze shifted.

A creak followed.

Then—snap.

A garland whip-lashed downward.

Julian's foot missed the beam.

And he fell.

The silence that followed wasn't shock.

It was *recognition.*

Because in a village this small, you always know the person who lands at your feet.

Chapter 2

No one moved.

The music had stopped somewhere between the snap and the fall, but the silence afterward was somehow louder.

Children froze mid-laugh. A dog barked once, then whimpered. The fluttering of the tent's garlands was the only sound for a full five seconds.

Then someone screamed.

And everything began to unravel.

"Is he—?"

"Call someone! Call the ambulance—has anyone called—?"

"He just—he slipped, right? It must've—"

Annabel didn't remember walking forward. Her feet did it for her, steady on instinct, stepping past the abandoned lemonade cups and half-packed prize baskets. Evie was beside her, one hand gripping a maypole ribbon like she might rip it down and throw it at whoever had let this happen.

Julian Parrish lay sprawled on the grass, limbs wrong in a way that made people turn away.

His scarf had landed like a flag beside him. One garland strand had followed, trailing like a snake over his leg.

And his eyes didn't move.

Annabel crouched beside him slowly. "Julian?" Her voice cracked. "Julian, can you hear me?"

No answer.

She reached out, gently. Fingers to his neck. No pulse.

She turned to the crowd. "He's not—" Her voice broke again.

But the ambulance siren was already wailing in the distance.

Julian Parrish had been, by all public accounts, the festival's golden son.

He could carve a heron out of driftwood with a spoon. He could tie a garland in fifteen minutes and still win the relay race after.

He'd won three craft categories, two strength events, and once wrote a haiku about rhubarb that made the parish vicar applaud.

People didn't just admire Julian.

They expected him.

He belonged to the festival.

To the crowd.

To Yewling, whose team he'd led every year with the kind of confidence that made mothers beam and rival villages bristle.

And now he was still.

Laid out in the centre of the square like a broken maypole.

Douglas Hartley, Little Firling's retired engineer and chief of unofficial village logic, stepped forward, squinting up at the garland.

"That knot's not right," he muttered. "Should've been reinforced with a secondary line. Steel, ideally."

Marigold Cresswell, Yewling's event coordinator and unofficial queen of bunting, let out a shaky breath. Her hands were clenched into her cardigan sleeves.

"He knew what he was doing," she said. "Julian was careful."

Behind her, Gareth Rowe — the mountain-sized woodworker and undefeated caber-toss champion — stood silently, jaw set. He had been

Julian's closest competitor, and in some ways, his shadow.

Mira Harrington, the sweet-natured baker from Firling who always brought extra for the judges, still held a tray of cinnamon buns she'd meant for the choir tent. One had slipped off the edge, frosting-down.

"I saw him this morning," she whispered. "He said the garlands were perfect this year. He smiled."

Celia Hargreaves, a retired librarian with an eye for scandal and an ear for whispers, narrowed her gaze at the tent ropes.

"Do we know who tied the top garland?" she asked, not to anyone in particular. "Because if it wasn't Julian..."

Evie cut in sharply. "Do we know why he was even up there again? Didn't he already check the garlands this morning?"

No one answered.

And then came Miles Parrish.

Julian's older brother. Quieter. More polished.

Less sunshine, more shadows in a suit.

He wasn't known for competing — but he attended every festival, every event, always watching from the edges.

People said he was "steady."

Annabel thought he was a locked box no one had ever found the key for.

He didn't rush to the body. Didn't cry. Didn't panic.

He just looked.

Then asked calmly, "Did anyone move him?"

He knelt beside Julian and closed his eyes with a hand that barely trembled.

Behind him hovered Bettany Marlowe, Little Firling's newly-returned florist, elegant even in grief. Her mouth formed no words. Her eyes didn't blink.

She clutched her scarf like a lifeline and watched Miles calmly.

Bernard Harper, the pub landlord and part-time poet, stood further back.

His arms crossed. His eyes flicking from the tent to his watch.

"This is going to ruin the schedule," he muttered. Then quickly added, "Poor lad."

Malcolm Ellis, the retired council treasurer from Little Yewling, was already walking the perimeter, clipboard in hand.

"Best we check the structure before anything else happens," he said mildly to no one in particular.

"I've got a list of who had access to the tents, if the officer wants it."

An hour later, the garland tent was cordoned off.

Children were ushered home.

Stalls packed away with nervous hands.

The music never resumed.

And in the silence, people began asking soft, nervous questions:

Why did Julian go back up the tent?

Who tied the garlands last?

Was it really just a fall?

"It was just an accident," Bernard repeated, as if saying it enough times would make it so.

Evie's voice was low but sharp. "One person goes up. One person falls. That's not maypole math."

Annabel didn't respond. Her gaze had drifted upward.

The tent still swayed slightly in the breeze. The garland Julian had touched fluttered loosely. Like it was trying to say something.

Persephone had not moved from beneath the tea stall.

But her eyes were locked on the empty air where Julian had once stood.

Chapter 3

The village square woke slowly.

The bunting fluttered half-heartedly in the morning breeze, some of it tangled where it had been left mid-pack down. Tables were still covered in crumbs and wrappers. A lone paper cup rolled across the cobblestones like it had nowhere to be.

Annabel stood at the edge of it all, cradling her mug of nettle tea.

Her roses were budding early — even the stubborn Desdemona had started to stretch herself skyward — but she couldn't quite feel spring this morning.

Across the square, the garland tent was cordoned off with red and white tape. The kind used for minor disruptions or suspiciously overbaked scones. But now it whispered something heavier: *keep out, truth being reassembled inside.*

Persephone padded across the grass, stopping only to sniff at a broken maypole ribbon still damp with dew.

Annabel watched her pause. Then paw gently at something in the grass.

A small knot of wood shavings and twine.

She knelt beside it, frowning. The garland Julian had been adjusting had used only pastel ribbon — this one was floral-printed, stiff with starch, and smelled faintly... sweet.

Like alyssum.

Like the orchard garlands. The ones stored three days ago.

She slipped it into her coat pocket as Evie approached, two takeaway coffees and a tabloid-level gleam in her eyes.

"You haven't heard the latest, have you?" she said, handing over a lukewarm latte.

Annabel sipped. "Please don't say Gareth's already blaming us."

"Too late. Yewling is *absolutely* crying foul. Marigold practically accused the entire WI of murder during sponge judging rechecks."

"And what do *we* think happened?"

Evie hesitated. Then:

"He didn't fall. He *was made to fall.*"

Annabel looked toward the tent again. "You sound awfully sure."

"Because PC Oakes is here. And he brought The Clipboard."

That was enough to draw a small gasp from Mira, who was just arriving with a tray of scones and nerves.

Inside the tent, PC Oakes stood near the central beam, his notebook in one hand and a pencil chewed halfway through.

He looked up as they approached. Cordial. Tired. Slightly flour-dusted, as if someone's baking had collided with his jumper.

"Ladies," he said. "Appreciate the space while we work. This is… well, this is not what we expected from the Harmony Festival."

Evie crossed her arms. "Is it true the beam was tampered with?"

PC Oakes paused, pencil tapping lightly against his wrist.

"Yes."

Just like that.

"Yes," he said again. "The screws anchoring the crossbeam were partially loosened. Clean work. Could've passed for weather damage if we hadn't found the scuff marks near the ladder base."

Annabel swallowed. "Scuff marks?"

"From a boot. Fresh. Julian's, likely. But we're trying to confirm. And we're also checking when the last inspection log was signed. Someone approved that tent as safe less than 48 hours ago."

Annabel's eyes slid to the side.

Malcolm Ellis, clipboard in hand, was speaking with a volunteer at the edge of the square. Calm. Helpful. Too helpful.

He wore the same beige windbreaker he wore for every village event — the kind that said "I have seen the accounts and I am not amused."

Evie whispered, "Why does he already look like he's briefing a jury?"

PC Oakes continued. "We'll be interviewing anyone with access to the tents this week. That includes organisers from both villages."

"Yewling's going to love that," Mira murmured.

And sure enough, Marigold Cresswell was storming up the path, hair immaculate, fury radiant.

"This is sabotage," she declared. "Plain and simple. And it's *your lot* who were in charge of floral installations yesterday!"

Annabel kept her voice even. "Julian tied most of the garlands himself. He was the only one allowed up that ladder."

"Exactly!" Marigold snapped. "So, who else had reason to adjust the beam after he approved it?"

Evie opened her mouth.

Annabel elbowed her before she could escalate.

Around them, the murmuring had begun.

***

"I *said* that tent looked unstable," came the sharp soprano of Mrs. Penelope Dawlish, arms crossed like a judgmental garden gnome. "But does anyone listen to Penelope? Nooo. Not until someone ends up horizontal in a flowerbed."

"That crossbeam doesn't just slip," said Trevor, from the hardware stall, to anyone who'd listen. "I built the bloody thing. Still good wood."

"I heard he was blackmailing someone," muttered *Stanley*, the village's most enthusiastic beekeeper and part-time conspiracy theorist. "Said so to my cousin's dog walker."

***

Celia Hargreaves hovered; notebook open like it was feeding her soul.

"Technically, this now qualifies as a suspicious death," she whispered to Mira.

"Which means I'll be updating my podcast notes."

Mira blinked. "You have a podcast?"

***

Gareth Rowe, looming by a lamppost, leaned in toward Miles Parrish — Julian's older brother, suit crisp, eyes unreadable.

"Julian should've stepped back this year," Gareth muttered. "He was tired."

Miles' voice was quiet, flat. "He never stepped back from anything. You know that."

***

Near the tea stand, two kids whispered: "Do you think the garlands are haunted now?"

"Only the purple ones."

***

Marigold stepped forward again, voice rising. "This isn't just a tragedy. It's foul play. And I don't think we've seen the last of it."

Evie, sweetly: "Gosh, I hope you saved your receipt for that bunting. Might need it for evidence."

***

Annabel turned away from the growing storm, the voices sharpening under bunting.

Persephone meowed from under the bench near the tent.

Then curled up tightly — right beneath the spot where Julian had landed.

No one spoke for a moment.

The garland above them fluttered again, like it was still trying to say something.

Chapter 4

The festival carried on.

Sort of.

A few events were quietly postponed. Others limped ahead with rearranged timings and tense smiles. The maypole was still up, but no one touched it. The garland tent was closed off like a crime scene—and technically, it was.

There were no announcements, just hushes. No brass band, just the occasional thud of someone putting down a tray too hard.

Annabel moved through the village square like it was a theatre between acts. People were gathered in small, whispering clusters, half-laughing too loudly or not at all. The bunting still fluttered, as if unaware one of the festival's brightest stars had just... fallen.

Persephone threaded silently through it all, nose twitching, tail flicking. Her expression hadn't changed since the fall—just cold calculation and the occasional disdainful blink. She paused near the tea tent, where someone had dropped a petal-wrapped note into the wrong bin.

Annabel sipped her tea, watching the crowd like it might confess something.

Evie slipped up beside her, her expression the human version of a raised eyebrow.

"Well," she said, "you won't believe who just re-materialised like a cursed ghost from a romantic subplot."

Annabel followed her line of sight—and froze.

At the far side of the square, near the floral tent, a woman in a cinched cream trench coat was adjusting a bouquet like she was doing a photo shoot. Oversized sunglasses. Glossed lips. Heels too sharp for village cobblestone.

"Who is *that?*" Annabel whispered.

Evie's grin went fox like.

"Vivienne Harrow."

(pause)

"Former fiancée to *both* Parrish brothers."

"Wait, really?"

"First Miles. Then Julian. Then no one, because he dumped her like cold toast in the middle of the Harmony Cup two years ago."

Annabel blinked. "And now she's back... helping with flowers?"

"She says she's *volunteering*," Evie said sweetly. "Which is adorable. Like saying you just *accidentally* wandered into your ex's murder investigation."

From the nearby bunting table, Mrs. Dawlish sniffed:

"She was on the television once. Coaching a pop star who cried during scales. Didn't see that coming."

Stanley the beekeeper added, "I thought she was dead."

Mira, passing by with another tray of consolation shortbread, muttered, "She still smells like expensive perfume and consequences."

Vivienne turned her head slowly, gaze sweeping the crowd from behind her sunglasses.

Then she looked directly at Miles Parrish.

He was standing near the tent line, talking with PC Oakes. His posture was still perfect. His expression unreadable. But his hands... his hands twitched once.

The air between them crackled.

Annabel felt it from across the square.

***

Later, Vivienne stepped behind the tea tent, ostensibly to retrieve more floral wire. Miles was already there. The tension snapped taut the moment they locked eyes.

"Still prefer grey suits, I see," she said, voice soft, polished.

"Still prefer theatrics," he replied.

A beat of silence.

The roses nearby leaned in. Even Persephone, watching from under a bench, didn't blink.

"You came back for him?" Miles asked.

Vivienne turned, slowly.

"I came back for myself."

(pause)

"And to remind myself why I left."

His jaw tightened.

"You left *for* him."

"And he left *me* in the rain with a broken heel and a borrowed umbrella."

(She smiled. It didn't reach her eyes.)

"Your brother had a talent for exits."

"He had a talent for everything," Miles said coolly.

"Except loyalty."

She stepped closer, just a little.

"Julian liked watching people fall, Miles. You, me... anyone who admired him too much."

(pause)

"He fell too, in the end."

She left him there, perfectly composed and utterly alone.

***

Meanwhile, secrets begin to shift...

Marigold Cresswell sniffed around the garland stall like a bloodhound, loudly declaring that "someone must have loosened that beam deliberately."

Gareth Rowe was seen muttering behind the tea stand, fists clenched. "He made a joke about my toss form. Called me a decorative tree stump in front of the judges."

Douglas Hartley quietly fixed a wobbling chair at the scone table and muttered to himself, "The beam was fine. He humiliated me for show. It was straight."

Celia Hargreaves updated her notebook every few minutes with the stealth of a spy.

Mira dropped a plate when someone said "Julian always made you feel special."

***

Persephone sat perfectly still beneath the bunting near the tent.

Watching.

Waiting.

The garland above fluttered again.

And someone else — someone quiet, someone unnoticed — slipped into the back of Julian's cottage with a key that shouldn't exist.

Chapter 5

Julian's cottage stood just past the stone footbridge that marked the invisible but *very real* boundary between Little Firling and Little Yewling.

The difference hit instantly.

Gone were the tangled hedges and mismatched lavender pots of Firling. Yewling's side was all crisp lines and manicured order. Garden borders were trimmed within an inch of their lives. The paving stones looked like they'd been chosen by a precision engineer, and every flowerbed bloomed as if someone had issued a formal schedule.

"You can always tell when you've crossed into Yewling," Evie muttered, "because the roses know better than to misbehave."

Julian's cottage was the final house before the path turned toward the green. It looked perfect from the outside—symmetrical, stylish, a little smug.

"Like him," Annabel said under her breath.

The front door stuck slightly as they entered. Inside, the air was cool. Still. Faint traces of bergamot, cedar polish, and the kind of cologne that tried too hard lingered in the air.

The space was everything Julian had always presented himself to be: curated, stylish, and filled with an exhausting number of perfectly arranged objects. Festival photos lined the walls, his trophy shelves gleamed, and a carved wooden kestrel sat mid-flight above the mantel like it was about to deliver passive-aggressive compliments.

But... something was off.

A drawer near the hallway table was left slightly ajar. A coaster had fallen behind the sofa. The rug beneath the desk was askew—just slightly, but in a house like this, that was its own kind of scream.

Evie bent beside the desk, frowning. "Someone's been in here."

"You mean apart from us?" Annabel asked softly.

"Yeah. And not like... grief-rummaging. Like, 'I have twenty seconds before someone sees me' energy."

Annabel opened a drawer. The files were shuffled, papers bent and unstacked. Someone had been searching.

But had they found what they wanted?

"If they were looking for something," she said, "they didn't stop to tidy up after."

"Which tells us they were scared. Or in a rush. Or both."

Persephone prowled under the table, tail flicking.

She sniffed at a stack of notebooks and meowed once—low and unimpressed—as if to say: *Amateurs.*

✳✳✳

Before arriving at Julian's cottage, Annabel and Evie have done their best to act casual while collecting gossip at the tea tent.

Gareth had been terse. "He made jokes. Always did. Called me 'The Yewling Oak.' Said I was more decorative than dangerous."

(He'd crushed a paper cup in one hand like it was nothing.)

"People laughed."

Marigold, in contrast, had performed grief like she was auditioning for local panto. "Julian was a pillar of our traditions," she said, lips trembling with precision. "And his garlands were... well. You couldn't ask for neater symmetry."

(Then, more quietly:)

"But he shouldn't have changed the scoring sheets. We agreed Mira's rose arch was runner-up."

(Pause.)

"Just... saying."

Mira had blinked back tears. "He was... lovely to me," she said. "Said I reminded him of someone. But he never explained who."

Douglas Hartley, the structural engineer who had once been mocked in front of the entire judges' table, had grunted:

"He rewrote my beam specs in front of six people. Said I was risking 'topple gate.' Then tied his own knots without checking tension. And now here we are."

Bernard Harper had remained breezy. "I was in the cellar with invoices," he insisted.

"That's funny," Mira had murmured. "You came through the tent right before the fall."

Bernard had smiled. "I've got a strong bladder. Doesn't mean I don't move fast."

***

Back at the cottage, Annabel moved a stack of neatly aligned ribbon boxes and found one more drawer underneath—deeper, older, and harder to notice unless you knew where to look.

It hadn't been touched.

She hesitated, then opened it.

Inside was a folder marked "*Festival 2024 – Storage + Floral*", but jammed behind it—clumsily hidden—was a plain envelope, slightly stained.

She opened it.

The letter was creased, handwritten in rushed, unfamiliar script. The ink had run in places. It was written in the first person—but without a name.

"I didn't mean to leave her. I just didn't know what to do. She said she was scared. That he'd made her promise not to tell. But I think he hurt her. I think... he hurt her more than once."

Tucked inside the folded page was a small silver locket.

Plain. No engraving.

Annabel opened the locket gently.

Two pressed flowers fluttered into her palm: alyssum and forget-me-not.

One soft and white, the other a faded blue, still clinging to its shape.

They looked delicate. Insignificant, almost. But something in Annabel's chest pulled tight.

"Alyssum," she murmured. "It means peace. Protection. It used to be called a cure for madness."

"Forget-me-not," Evie whispered beside her. "Remembrance. Loyalty. The need to be remembered."

They weren't just decoration.

They were a message.

A whisper from someone who had been hurt. Or lost. Or left behind.

Someone who wanted—no, *needed*—to be remembered.

Annabel turned the locket over.

There, etched faintly into the back of the clasp, just visible in the light:

Iris.

They stared at each other.

"Who's Iris?" Annabel asked.

Evie shook her head slowly. "I don't know. But I think Julian did."

Persephone padded forward and sniffed the flowers, tail flicking once, twice.

She looked up at them both, and then turned her gaze to the cottage window.

Outside, the sun had started to shift—casting long, delicate shadows across Little Yewling's perfect paving stones.

Inside, the name lingered.

Iris.

Chapter 6

The ribbons were still up. But no one looked at them.

Festival events had resumed—technically. The maypole stood untouched, the bake-off was missing three judges, and the tug-of-war rope sat coiled in the corner of the green like it was grieving.

People smiled too tightly. Spoke too softly. And behind every sentence was the same question:

If Julian didn't fall... who made him?

Annabel and Evie returned from the cottage with the locket carefully wrapped in a handkerchief, and silence between them as thick as clotted cream. Persephone trailed behind, tail high, like a one-cat funeral procession.

"So," Evie finally said as they passed the noticeboard, "do we tell PC Oakes we found a letter that might reference a crime, hidden behind Julian's floral maps? Or do we... wait to be arrested with dignity?"

Annabel didn't answer. She was still thinking about the flowers.

***

In Little Firling, Douglas Hartley was seen hammering down a loose tent peg— aggressively. Too aggressively. When someone offered help, he waved them off with a grunt and muttered, "If Julian hadn't rewritten my safety specs, he might've still—never mind."

Mira walked through the square in silence, eyes puffy. Her tray of fig tarts had burned that morning.

Marigold loudly accused someone— *anyone*—of "tampering with her rose wreath entry."

"You can't just MOVE someone's centre bloom! That's artistic assault!"

Gareth was seen leaving the village hall storage shed in a hurry.

He said he was "just checking rope tension."

No one believed him.

✳✳✳

It was Celia who said it first.

She was flipping through the *Little Yewling Historical Society scrapbook* (her version of light reading) when she paused.

"Iris," she said softly, to no one in particular. "That name hasn't come up in a while."

Annabel, passing by with a tray of tea and stress-shortbread, froze.

"You know the name?"

Celia tilted her head.

"She volunteered for the floral tent last year. Bit shy. Always had lilac ink on her hands."

"Where is she now?"

"Vanished. Summer festival, just after the judging. Some say she moved. But no forwarding address. No goodbye."

She looked up from the scrapbook.

"Julian knew her well."

***

Evie began assembling a notebook of timelines, motives, and inconsistencies— color-coded, with doodles.

"I'm telling you," she said as they walked toward the tearoom, "someone's lying about their whereabouts during tent setup. Douglas? Nervous. Bernard? Full-on shifting timelines like chairs in a fire drill. Gareth? Tension in the shoulders. Screams 'I hate being second-best.'"

Persephone leapt onto the bench beside them, sniffed the locket, and turned her back on it dramatically.

"She disapproves," Annabel said.

"Of Julian, the killer, or my graphing skills?"

"All three."

***

Annabel had always thought Gillian Marsh's cottage, tucked just beyond the orchard path, was the most peaceful spot in Little Firling.

Quiet. Bloom-heavy. Safe.

Until now.

That night, from her bedroom window, Annabel spotted a flicker of movement across the green.

Gillian. In her own garden.

She wasn't watering. Or weeding at this hour.

She was crouched near the back rose bed, holding something in her hands—dark, crumpled. A moment later, a thin ribbon of smoke rose into the evening air.

Annabel narrowed her eyes.

"What is she burning?" she whispered.

Behind her, Persephone leapt onto the windowsill and let out a soft, warning growl.

Chapter 7

The festival carried on like a party that had forgotten what it was celebrating.

Children still raced across the green, but their laughter rang too loudly. The bunting still fluttered, but now it looked frayed, a little desperate. A scone was dropped at the bake-off table and no one even gasped.

And in the middle of it all, the villagers were beginning to turn on each other.

✳ ✳ ✳

Gareth Rowe was spotted dragging crates from the tug-of-war shed with enough force to threaten the structural integrity of the shed itself. When Annabel and Evie approached, he barely grunted a greeting.

"You were close with Julian, weren't you?" Evie asked.

"Close like vinegar to a wound."

Annabel raised an eyebrow.

"You ever see him with Iris? Last year?"

He hesitated. Just a beat too long.

"She was always around. Bit clingy. Thought he was a god. He treated her like she was lucky to breathe the same air."

His jaw twitched.

"He liked to see people fall."

***

Marigold Cresswell was in full crisis-prep mode. She'd redone the entire rose garland "in honour of Julian," while also hinting that her original design was stolen... by Julian... while alive.

"Honestly, I think the man's still rearranging things from the grave."

Evie muttered, "He's haunting the judging sheets."

***

Bernard Harper couldn't keep his story straight.

"I was restocking gin in the back."

"You said you were logging beer yesterday."

"Did I?" he smiled. "It's all in the paperwork."

Only, the paperwork was *missing.*

Mira quietly said he wasn't in the pub until *after* the fall.

She wouldn't look anyone in the eye while she said it.

***

That afternoon, Annabel ran into Douglas Hartley behind the tea tent. He looked tired, but more focused than usual. He carried a sketchpad and tapped it nervously with a pen.

"I've been looking at the tent again. The way it came down. It's bothering me."

"Because of Julian's changes?"

"No... because of something I saw. The day before. Near the supply stack."

He looked over her shoulder, distracted.

"There was someone there. Not from the team. I just assumed they were helping but—"

He stopped.

"It wasn't right. I think I... no. Let me check something first. I'll ring you."

Annabel opened her mouth to press, but he was already walking away.

***

Annabel missed his call. Her phone was inside while she was in the garden. Evie was arguing with Celia about missing bunting.

By the time she checked it, there was a voicemail. She pressed play.

Douglas's voice crackled through, soft and breathless.

"Annabel. I think I've got it. The one at the tent—he wasn't supposed to be there. I—I can't remember the face, but I remember... I saw blue — a sleeve, just slipping past the rope before the tent gave way—."

The message ended abruptly.

The time stamp was twenty minutes ago.

***

They found him just before dusk.

Behind the supply tent, near a collapsed stack of garland poles.

PC Oakes stood beside the body, face pale, hands gloved. He picked up one of the poles. Blood stained the end.

"One blow to the back of the head," he said grimly. "Stack was knocked after."

"To make it look like an accident?" Annabel asked.

Oakes nodded slowly.

"This wasn't an accident."

Persephone sat nearby, still and alert. Her tail was wrapped around her paws like a noose.

She was staring not at the body, but at the corner of the tent.

Where someone had left a footprint.

Small.

Precise.

Not Douglas's.

Chapter 8

The village square had emptied faster than anyone remembered.

No music. No ribbon practice. The maypole stood still, fluttering gently in the evening breeze like a dancer waiting for a partner who would never arrive.

Children were kept indoors.

One moment they were chasing each other through bunting and half-eaten pastries, and the next, mothers were calling names from doorways with trembling voices. Cakes were left uneaten.

The Harmony Cup sat under a sheet like a relic of a festival that had forgotten how to celebrate.

Mr. Latham from the post office locked the front gate of the village green. No one argued.

By teatime, Little Firling had stopped pretending things were fine.

Two deaths in three days.

One from Yewling. One from Firling.

Both part of the festival.

Someone finally said what they were all thinking.

"This isn't an accident. This is a pattern."

***

Marigold Cresswell sobbed loudly over her rose display, claiming "the festival was cursed" and that *"the symmetry gods are angry."*

Celia muttered that this was *"just like the 1908 incident,"* though the only similarity was a floral scandal and a broken ankle.

Bernard stood behind his pub stall looking pale and defensive, arms crossed like a man preparing to be accused. Again.

Mira had vanished.

And PC Oakes?

He was speaking to every committee member in rotation — slow, quiet conversations followed by a lot of notepad scribbling.

✳✳✳

A small group of Yewling villagers stood clustered near the Harmony Cup, arms folded tight, voices low.

"Julian was one of ours."

"And now Douglas — from here — is dead too."

"What if someone from Firling... retaliated?"

"What if it's someone from *our side* trying to stir things up?"

Evie passed by the group and heard the words "serial killer" spoken with the cautious awe of people who secretly wanted to say it louder.

"This is ridiculous," she hissed to Annabel. "This isn't the BBC. It's bunting and jam and secrets. It's not *Netflix*."

"It's murder," Annabel said softly. "And someone's hiding in plain sight."

***

That's when they saw her.

Persephone, slinking across the green like she had personally declared a state of emergency.

Tail high. Steps deliberate. No fear in her eyes — just that cool, calculating glint that made people uneasy even on a normal day.

She stopped beside the judging tent, looked back at Annabel and Evie, and gave a single meow.

Then she padded behind the structure and sat.

Waiting.

"Oh no," Evie whispered. "She's doing the thing. The clue thing."

"She's *never* done the clue thing this soon."

Annabel and Evie followed her around the back.

Tucked in the grass behind the tent stake was a scrap of paper.

Crinkled. Dirt-stained.

And unmistakably torn from a notebook.

Annabel crouched. It was smudged with a thumbprint, faded from rain, but still legible.

Just three words, scrawled in pencil:

"*I saw her.*"

***

The crowd had thinned, but the tension hadn't.

Celia stood near the bake-off tent, arms folded, eyes sharp behind her glasses.

"First Julian. Now Douglas," she said, not bothering to whisper. "And they weren't even close. You don't kill two people unless they've got something in common."

"Unless," added Bernard, appearing from nowhere like all good pub owners do, "someone had something *against* them. The same person, maybe."

"Do you think they knew something?" said a younger villager, wringing her hands. "Or... someone *thought* they did?"

"Julian had no enemies," Marigold huffed. "Apart from everyone he ever spoke to."

PC Oakes had overheard. He turned toward them, arms crossed.

"We're not ruling anything out," he said. "But until we know why Douglas was killed, we can't say whether this is about Julian. Or something else entirely."

He glanced at Annabel.

"Did Douglas mention anything odd to you? Anything worth... killing over?"

Annabel hesitated.

"He said he saw someone. Someone who shouldn't have been near the tent."

"Did he say who?"

"No," she whispered. "But he was going to."

***

They didn't say the words out loud, but the note burned behind their eyes.

I saw her.

The green buzzed with paranoia. People gave each other long; lingering looks like strangers at a murder mystery dinner party who suddenly remembered the menu was poisoned.

Even Mira wasn't spared.

Someone muttered, "She was always close to Julian. Too close."

Marigold nodded far too eagerly.

Bernard said nothing — but *stared,* and that said more.

"This is stupid," Evie hissed. "Mira's barely said ten words all year."

"Maybe someone wants us to look at the wrong person," Annabel replied.

***

Vivienne appeared at the edge of the tea tent, arms crossed, voice quieter than usual

"There was a girl," she said softly. "Last summer. The day I came back to collect a box of my mum's things."

Annabel turned.

"What kind of girl?"

"Young. Sweet face. I didn't speak to her. But I remember Julian—"

(She hesitated.)

"He was talking to her near the orchard stall. Too close. His hand was on her back like he was steadying her... but she wasn't moving."

She shook her head.

"She looked like she wanted to vanish. I never saw her again."

***

Behind them, Gillian walked past with a tray of tea and a scarf wound tightly around her wrist like it was the only thing holding her together.

She didn't look at anyone.

Persephone turned her head, eyes tracking her with laser precision.

"She's been so quiet lately," someone muttered.

Annabel didn't reply.

***

The crowd scattered again, slower this time. Everyone pretending they weren't imagining themselves as the next headline.

Annabel stared at the note in her hand.

Three words. A world of trouble.

I saw her.

But who was "her"?

And what had she been seen doing?

***

Gillian sat at her dressing table, the lamplight catching the silver chain at her throat. The locket had been hers for years — a simple oval, not unlike the one her sister used to wear. She turned it absently between her fingers, as if the cool metal might answer back. And for a fleeting second remembered Iris fastening a silver hairpin into her dark hair, its tiny forget-me-nots catching the light.

What if Iris had been right all along?

Gillian had dismissed her sister's trembling words as nerves, or the restlessness of a young wife married to an older man. Malcolm had seemed steady, respectable — if exacting. Gillian told herself Iris simply wasn't suited to him.

But now, looking into her own eyes in the mirror, she saw doubt instead of certainty.

What if Iris had been followed? Controlled? And I refused to listen?

The locket clicked shut in her hand.

What if my silence cost her everything?

Chapter 9

Voices rose and fell in soft, scandalized huddles. The kind of volume you use when you want everyone to *overhear you pretending to whisper.*

"I always thought Douglas had a look about him," said Bernard, polishing a glass like it had wronged him. "Quiet, mysterious... that's the type who keeps secrets."

"You think he was having an *affair?*" Marigold gasped.

"With *who?*"

"Well," Bernard said, smug, "someone saw her."

"What 'her'?" Marigold's hands were already on her hips. "You think *I* was—?!"

"He never missed your lemon drizzle submission."

"That's because it's excellent!"

Evie passed by with a teacup and muttered under her breath, "Pretty sure he was more loyal to cake than anyone's petticoat."

Vivienne, perched near the edge of the crowd, sipped her lemonade slowly.

"If Douglas had a secret romance, I'll personally eat Marigold's award-winning jam. All of it. With a spoon."

Celia chimed in helpfully:

"He once borrowed a historical romance novel and never returned it. Maybe it was research."

The conversation spun itself like a carousel, turning faster with every pass.

By the time PC Oakes wandered by, someone was earnestly suggesting Douglas had been in love with a librarian from Dorset and murdered in a tragic long-distance crime of passion.

Annabel blinked.

"Or..." she said gently, "it could've been something he *saw.* You know. Something worth killing for."

The group quieted. Briefly. Then Marigold sniffed.

"That seems far less romantic."

***

The cottage smelled of damp stone and old tobacco. Annabel shifted a pile of notebooks, and beneath them found an envelope, flattened and discoloured with age. There was no stamp, no address — just paper folded inside, tucked away and forgotten.

She opened it carefully. The ink wavered across the page, uneven as though written in haste:

I don't know who this is for.
Maybe no one. Maybe just the wall.
But if someone finds this...

I want you to know I was here.

Evie leaned closer.

He told me I was special.
Then he said I was his.
And when I tried to pull away, he
said someone else would pay the price.
I didn't believe him.
Not until I saw his eyes change.
Not until he started watching her.

The last line ended in a blot of ink, the pen dragged down the page.

Annabel swallowed. "It reads like she stopped mid-thought. Or couldn't go on."

She folded the paper back into its envelope with care. "Hidden, not sent. Just a trace in case silence swallowed her completely."

The cottage seemed to breathe around them, heavy with absence. Persephone leapt onto the table, paw resting lightly against the paper, as though marking it.

***

Silence stretched between them.

Evie swallowed hard. "She knew that something was not right."

Annabel folded the letter with trembling fingers. "She wrote like someone waiting to be believed."

"And it seems that someone made sure she never was," Vivienne said from the doorway.

They turned. She hadn't knocked.

She held the locket in her hand.

The one Annabel had found and that she has placed on the table.

The one with the photo of a girl smiling with uncertainty tucked behind pressed alyssum and forget-me-not.

Vivienne's voice cracked.

"That's her. That's the girl I saw with Julian last summer."

"You're sure?" Annabel asked.

Vivienne nodded slowly.

"He touched her like she was a possession. And she looked like a bird trying not to breathe too loud."

***

She has heard about the locket, she has heard the name of Iris spoken aloud - and the letter, even if she hasn't read it, felt like a reckoning.

She doesn't know what happened to her sister, but she knows that she has helped to cover something up and she has believed someone who told her not to ask questions,

And now... *the truth is coming for her.*

***

Outside, the orchard trees shifted in the breeze, their branches creaking like they were remembering something.

Persephone pressed her face to the window, ears twitching, eyes locked on a familiar shape in the distance.

On the bench near the path sat Gillian.

Still. Hands clenched around another similar locket.

Her lips moved like she was whispering a name she hadn't said aloud in years.

Not crying. Not yet.

Just... realizing.

Persephone flicked her tail once.

The garden held its breath.

***

Mira sat in her kitchen long after the kettle had gone cold.

Outside, the wind had picked up, tugging at the windowpanes like a memory trying to get in. The festival green lay in silence, its garlands drooping in the dark.

The folded paper on her table hadn't moved in over a year.

Not since Iris gave it to her.

She hadn't opened it.

She wasn't supposed to.

"Just in case," Iris had said softly, the words nearly lost under the rustle of flower stems.

"In case I leave. Or in case someone tries to say I didn't matter."

Mira had promised.

She hadn't read it.

Not even when Iris vanished.

She thought about it sometimes—when the village got too loud, when Julian laughed too hard, when Gillian stopped making eye contact. But she had held back.

Until now.

Now that another letter was found in Julian's cottage.

Now Iris' name was being said again, not just whispered in back rooms.

Now... it was time.

***

She touched the envelope like it might crumble under her fingers. The edges were soft with age. A little flower—an alyssum bloom, pressed and faded—was tucked inside.

She unfolded the note.

It wasn't long.

It didn't need to be.

Mira stared at the words until they blurred.

Iris had known.

Maybe not everything.

But enough.

Enough to write this.

Enough to trust someone would listen.

***

She folded the paper carefully, hands trembling.

Tomorrow, she would do what Iris had asked.

She would tell the truth.

Even if it hurt.

Especially if it did.

Outside, the orchard trees rustled like they were waking up.

And in the darkness, the village held its breath.

Chapter 10

The orchard was cloaked in the soft hues of twilight, the air thick with the scent of blooming alyssum. Gillian sat alone on the weathered bench beneath the ancient oak, her fingers tracing the delicate contours of her locket that rested heavily in her palm. Looking at the locket reminded her of Iris' laughter and later of her withdrawal. The distant murmur of the festival drifted through the trees, a stark contrast to the turmoil that churned within her.

Persephone, ever the silent sentinel, perched gracefully at her feet, her emerald eyes reflecting the fading light.

The crunch of footsteps on gravel broke the stillness. Annabel and Evie emerged from the shadows; their faces etched with concern and quiet determination.

Annabel approached cautiously; her voice gentle yet probing.

"Gillian, we've been looking for you. The festival... it's not the same without you."

Gillian's gaze remained fixed on the locket, her voice barely above a whisper.

"She used to love this time of year. Iris ... my sister. The festival was her sanctuary."

Evie stepped closer; her brow furrowed.

"Iris... your sister?"

A bitter smile played at the corners of Gillian's lips.

"Yes. She had a way of finding beauty in the chaos."

Annabel exchanged a glance with Evie before speaking again.

"Gillian, we found something. Among Julian's belongings."

She extended a folded piece of paper, its edges worn with time and the locket that was found. Gillian hesitated before taking them, her fingers trembling as she unfolded the note.

The note found in Julian's cottage sent a shiver down her spine.

Tears welled in Gillian's eyes as the weight of the words settled upon her heart.

"I should have known," she murmured. "She tried to tell me, in her own way. But I was blind."

Evie knelt beside her, her voice soft yet insistent.

"Tell us, Gillian. What happened?"

Gillian took a shuddering breath, the memories cascading over her like a tidal wave.

"Iris came to me, not long before she vanished. She was... different. Frightened. She spoke of shadows that followed her, of feeling trapped. I dismissed her fears, chalked it up to her overactive imagination."

She clenched Iris' locket tightly, as if seeking solace from its cold surface.

"Then she disappeared. No note, no goodbye. Just... gone. And I believed Malcolm when he said she needed time, that she'd return when she was ready."

Annabel's voice was laced with gentle scepticism.

"And now?"

Gillian's eyes burned with unshed tears.

"Now I see the cracks. The inconsistencies. Julian tried to confront Malcolm, and then he was gone too. And Douglas... he mentioned seeing something, someone near the tent that day. A blue sleeve."

Evie's eyes widened.

"Malcolm's coat."

A heavy silence settled over them, the unspoken implications hanging in the air like a storm cloud.

The distant chime of the festival bell broke the spell. Gillian rose to her feet, her resolve hardening.

"I need to find Malcolm. I need answers."

Annabel placed a reassuring hand on her arm.

"We'll stand by you, Gillian. You're not alone in this."

Gillian offered a grateful nod, her heart pounding with a mix of fear and determination.

As they made their way back toward the heart of the festival, Persephone trailed behind, her keen eyes ever watchful.

Chapter 11

The morning after Gillian broke in the orchard, the village wasn't quite the same.

Little Firling and Little Yewling hadn't agreed to cancel the remaining Harmony Festival events, but they didn't feel celebratory either. The garlands stayed up, but the music was quieter. The cakes were cut with fewer smiles.

Something had shifted.

And in that hush, Mira came to Honeystone Cottage.

*   *   *

Annabel opened the door to find Mira. Her apron was dusted in flour again, but her eyes were different—less glassy, more focused, as though she'd finally finished the sentence she'd been carrying for years.

"I didn't know who else to tell," she said softly.

Annabel lowered the ribbon she was holding. "Tell me what?"

"Iris gave me this," Mira whispered. "One evening, just before the festival that year. She looked frightened. Not angry, not sad—frightened. Said only: *keep it safe.*

I never read it. Thought it wasn't my place."

Annabel unfolded the brittle paper. The handwriting tilted, hurried. Only a few lines remained:

If anything happens to me, it was not an accident.

Someone wanted me silent.

Please don't believe everything you hear.

Evie's breath caught. "She knew that something would happen."

Mira nodded slowly. "She did. And Julian... he knew something too."

She reached again into her pocket and pulled out a slightly creased photograph.

"Julian gave this to me a few days before the fall. Said if anything happened to him, I should show someone."

Annabel took the photo. It was grainy. A patch of earth, uneven, scattered with disturbed leaves and the faint suggestion of fabric. Blue. Faded.

"Julian said a dog had been digging in the back of Malcolm's garden. He thought he saw the edge of fabric—pink and pale green, with tiny flowers. He didn't know what it meant... but he knew it wasn't right."

Her voice cracked. "I think... I think someone buried something."

Evie leaned in. "That looks like a dress."

Mira nodded, slowly. "He told me it looked like something Iris would have worn."

The room fell still. Persephone sat on the windowsill, tail twitching once. Watching.

***

PC Oakes stood in Malcolm's garden half an hour later, holding the photo against the overcast light. The garden smelled sharp — rosemary, wet ivy, just-cut grass. Everything was tidy. Just like Malcolm liked it.

The photo pointed to the patch just behind the fence line.

Oakes picked up a spade.

"Let's start here."

Annabel, Evie, and Mira watched from the side. Gillian stayed further back, hands in her coat pockets, expression unreadable.

Malcolm stood with arms crossed, unmoved.

Oakes dug.

The earth came up damp and dark. Shovelful after shovelful.

Nothing.

No cloth.

No bones.

Just silence.

"Is this what we're doing now?" Malcolm said, voice calm.

"Turning gardens into graveyards because of a rumour?"

Evie shot him a look.

"Funny. You're not asking who or what we think is buried."

Oakes frowned.

"The photo matches. But there's nothing here."

A long pause.

Then a soft sound:

A footfall.

***

Persephone stepped through the hedge. Quiet. Intentional.

She walked past the hole. Past Oakes. Past Malcolm.

And went into a lush bloom of bluebells along the edge of the shed — ten feet to the right of where they were digging.

She sniffed.

Scratched once.

Then sat.

Still.

Malcolm's face twitched.

"Get her out of there."

He stepped forward, hand out, trying to push her away.

Persephone didn't move.

She hissed.

A low, guttural warning.

And then she arched her back and dug a single paw into the soil.

Bluebells fell aside.

Annabel's voice was soft:

"She knows."

Oakes lowered the spade.

"There."

***

The digging started again. Slower. Deeper.

The spade scraped against stone. Then fabric. A floral print, faded by soil but still visible — pink, pale green, flowers tangled with roots.

Oakes froze. For a long moment, no one moved. The orchard held its breath.

Carefully, he brushed aside the dirt and lifted something small, glinting faintly in the lamplight. A silver hairpin, with at its base a motif with tiny forget-me-nots.

Gillian's hand flew to her mouth. Her voice broke into a whisper. "That was Iris's."

The orchard seemed to grow colder. The fabric, the bones, the little flower in silver — together, they told the truth at last.

***

Malcolm didn't speak when the cuffs were brought out.

He didn't resist.

But as they led him down the path, he turned to Gillian.

"You always believed me."

Her eyes didn't waver.

"I believed what you let me see."

***

Later, as the sun dipped low and the bluebells stirred in the wind, Mira placed the photo and Iris' scarf in a small tin beneath the orchard tree.

Gillian laid a single forget-me-not beside it.

Persephone curled on the bench above. Watching.

The village, at last, exhaled.

Epilogue

The Harmony Cup sat slightly crooked on its pedestal, the silver a little more tarnished than anyone admitted out loud — but it gleamed just the same.

The final ceremony was quieter this year. No speeches. No confetti.

Just Nora from the tea tent blinking back tears as she handed the trophy to Mira.

"For the lavender and lemon curd tart," she said, voice thick.

"And for reminding us how to tell the truth."

Mira didn't cry. But she smiled — small, soft, and real.

Little Firling and Little Yewling had called a truce. Officially.

They still muttered about scorekeeping. But the maypole was shared this year — ribbons criss-crossed from both villages, tied by children who didn't care about old rivalries, only the way the wind caught the silk and made it dance.

Evie had somehow won the "most artistic bunting arrangement" category.

"I didn't even enter," she whispered to Annabel.

"You did," Annabel said, sipping tea. "You just forgot."

Persephone was curled on the edge of the tea table, watching the entire event like she was silently judging every jam entry.

Which, of course, she was.

***

At the orchard, Gillian came once. Quietly. Alone.

She knelt by the tree where Iris had once breathed her last — *not where she was buried now*, but the place where something of her still lingered in the wind, in the soil, in the silence that came before the fall.

She placed a small tin beneath the bench.

Inside were a pressed forget-me-not, a few alyssum petals, and a folded piece of paper that said nothing. Because some griefs speak best in silence.

"They moved you," she whispered. "But I'll always return here. Because this is where you still bloom."

Then she rose and walked away — not vanishing, just returning to a world that had cracked, and now, maybe, could begin again.

***

Back at Honeystone Cottage, the garden had never looked more alive.

The Desdemona roses were opening in pale-pink glory.

The Double Delights were already being too dramatic.

And the New Dawn was climbing higher than it had last spring — like it knew it had more to see this time.

Inside, the kettle whistled.

Evie was drawing suspicious lines through her "Cozy Crime Case Tracker."

"One day," she said to Annabel, "someone's going to write a book about this."

"Just one?"

"Maybe a trilogy."

They clinked mugs.

Persephone sat on the windowsill, gaze fixed on the garden, tail twitching once.

The wind stirred the lavender.

And somewhere beyond the square, the last maypole ribbon fluttered free — caught for a second, then drifting slowly back to earth.

About the Author

Belinda writes layered mysteries where memory lingers, landscapes remember, and silence speaks louder than words. Her stories slip between the literary and the intimate—part atmospheric suspense, part quiet reckoning. Rooted in a love for islands, history, and hidden truths, her work invites readers to linger in the in-between.

She believes some lands carry echoes of everything they've witnessed—grief, joy, betrayal—and that nostalgia for a place is its own kind of story.

She also writes heartfelt children's stories that whisper courage into quiet hearts. With magical ladybugs, story-saving oaks, and brave little girls like Maia, Belinda hopes to help young readers find their own voice—and use it boldly.

When she's not writing, Belinda tends to her garden, guided by the rustle of leaves, the smell of earth, and the quiet company of two cats who always seem to know more than they let on.